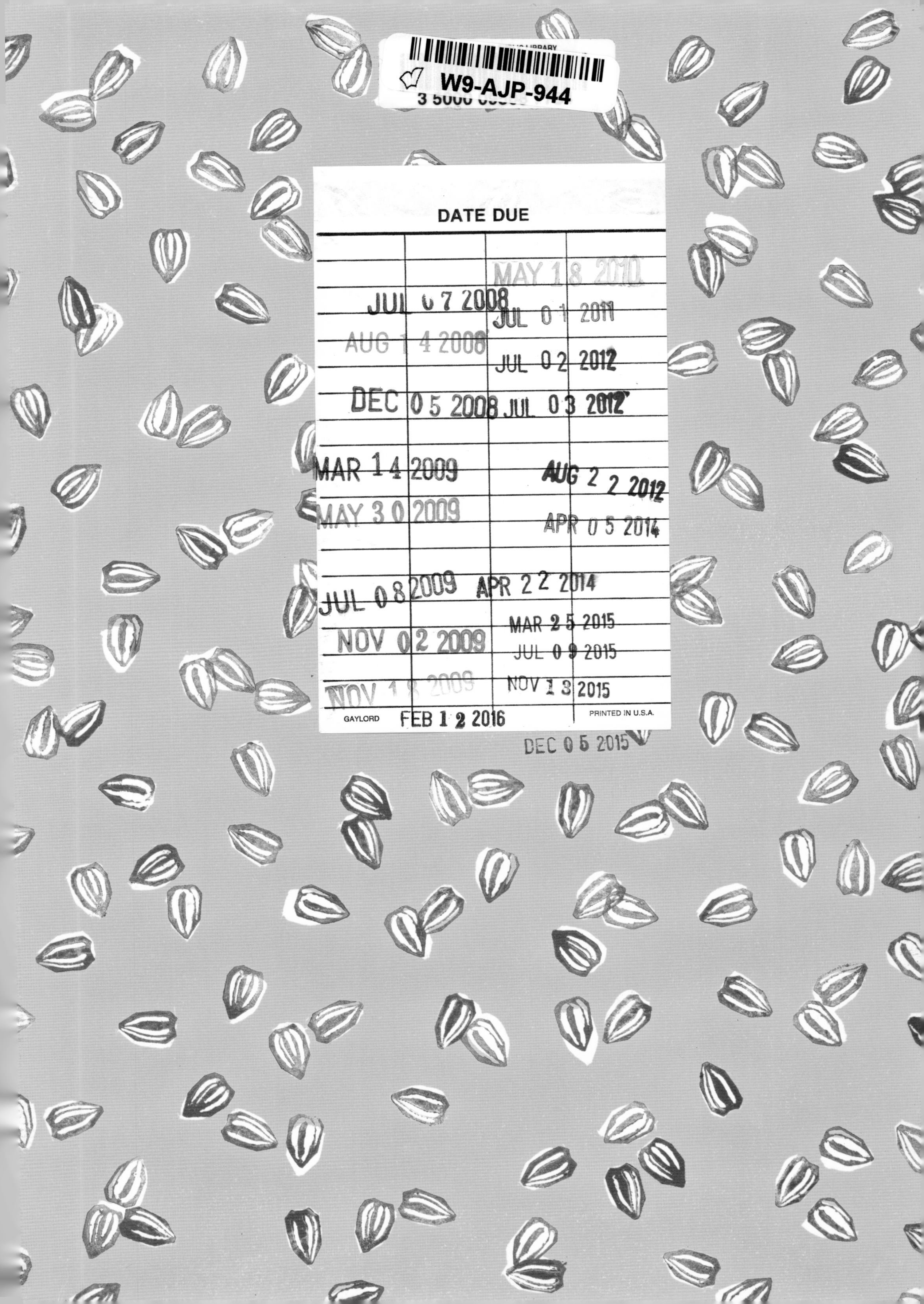

to be like the SUN

Harcourt, Inc.
Orlando Austin New York San Diego

www.HarcourtBooks.com

Portions of the text previously published as the poem "To Be Like the Sun" in *Getting Used to the Dark: 26 Night Poems,* DK Publishing, Inc., 1997.

Library of Congress Cataloging-in-Publication Data
Swanson, Susan Marie.
To be like the sun/Susan Marie Swanson;
Margaret Chodos-Irvine.
p. cm.
Summary: A child reflects on how a small, striped gray seed eventually becomes a strong, beautiful sunflower.
[1. Seeds—Fiction. 2. Sunflowers—Fiction.]
I. Chodos-Irvine, Margaret, ill. II. Title.
PZ7.S97255Tob 2008
[E]—dc22 2006103262
ISBN 978-0-15-205796-1

First edition
H G F E D C B A

Manufactured in China

The illustrations in this book were created using a variety of nontraditional printmaking techniques and materials.
The display type was set in Granby Opti Elephant Condensed.
The text type was set in Futura.
Color separations by Bright Arts Ltd., Hong Kong
Manufactured by South China Printing Company, Ltd., China
Production supervision by Pascha Gerlinger
Designed by Margaret Chodos-Irvine
and Michele Wetherbee

For my brothers,
David and Bruce, and their families
—S. M. S.

For my brother, Jon, and his family
—M. C.-I.

Hello, little seed,
striped gray seed.
Do you really know everything
about sunflowers?

My hoe breaks apart
the clods of brown earth,
but you do the real work
down in the dark.

Not radish work or pumpkin,
not thistle work—
sunflower work.
All the instructions
are written in your heart.

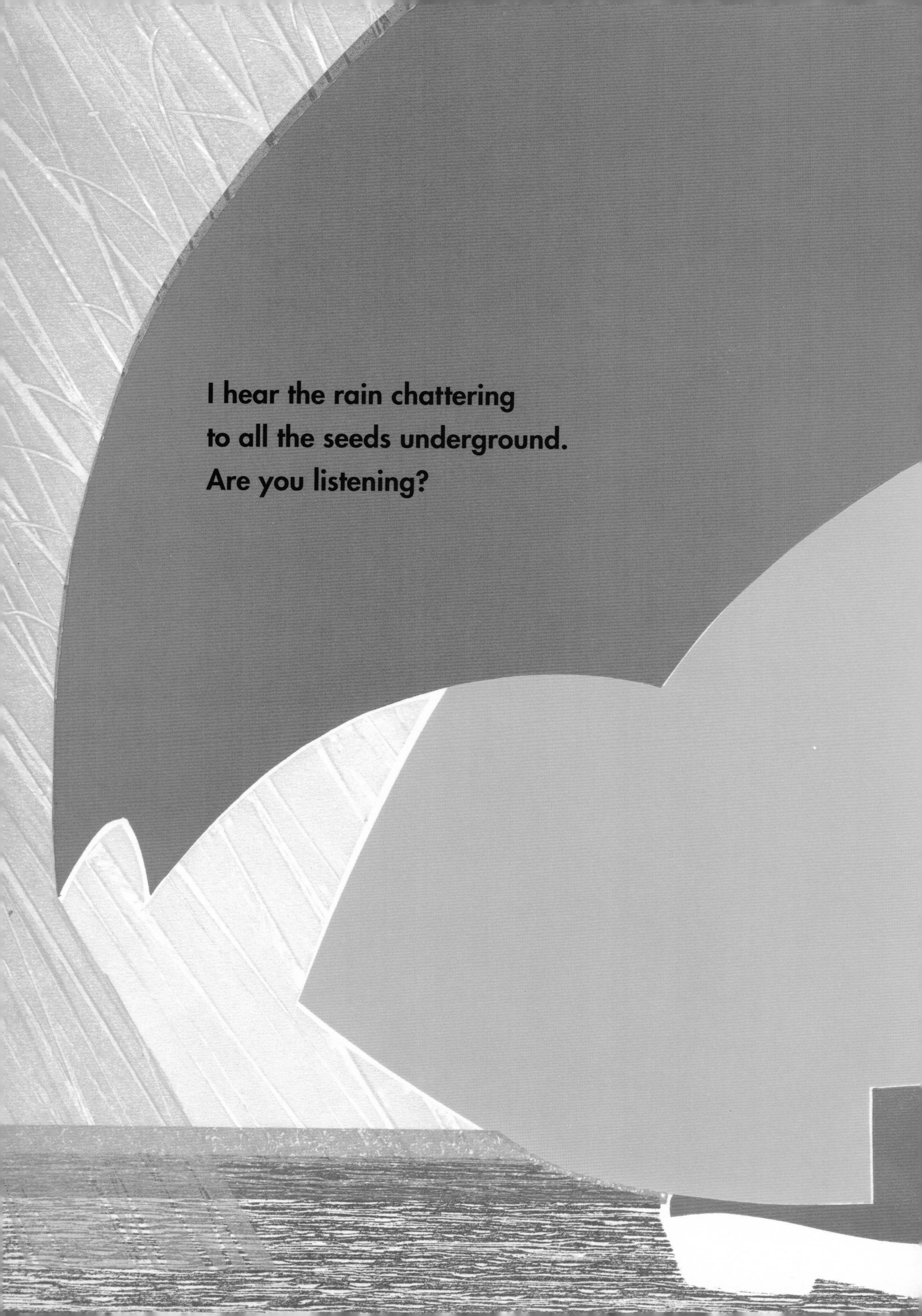

I hear the rain chattering
to all the seeds underground.
Are you listening?

I can’t hear you say
anything back.

Sunflower,
when you found your way
out of the ground,
you looked hard at the sun.

You made roots and leaves,
then stem,

more leaves,
more roots,

stem,

then a bud
like hands closed tight
around a treasure.

The days keep getting longer
and greener
and hotter.

I drag a long hose
across the grass
so you can drink.

Now you've made your own sun
up over my head!

The whole world wants to be golden
like you, sunflower,
to rest in the cool air
at sunset,
listening to cricket songs,

looking at the place
where the sun goes down,
thinking about the sun
even when it has gone away.

All these seeds—are you tired
of holding them up?
What makes them so heavy?
Is it light caught inside?
There are so many—
more than all the days
of summer.

The wind rattles
in the garden, tattering
old leaves and stems.
Cold wind rocks our bird feeder
filled with little seeds,
striped gray sunflower seeds.

Sunflower,
we taped a snapshot of you
to our refrigerator.

Your picture
is smaller than my hand,

and a sunflower seed
is smaller than a word,

but I remember:
you were taller than everyone.
When the winter sky shivers
with icy stars,
I remember how hard you worked

to be like the sun.

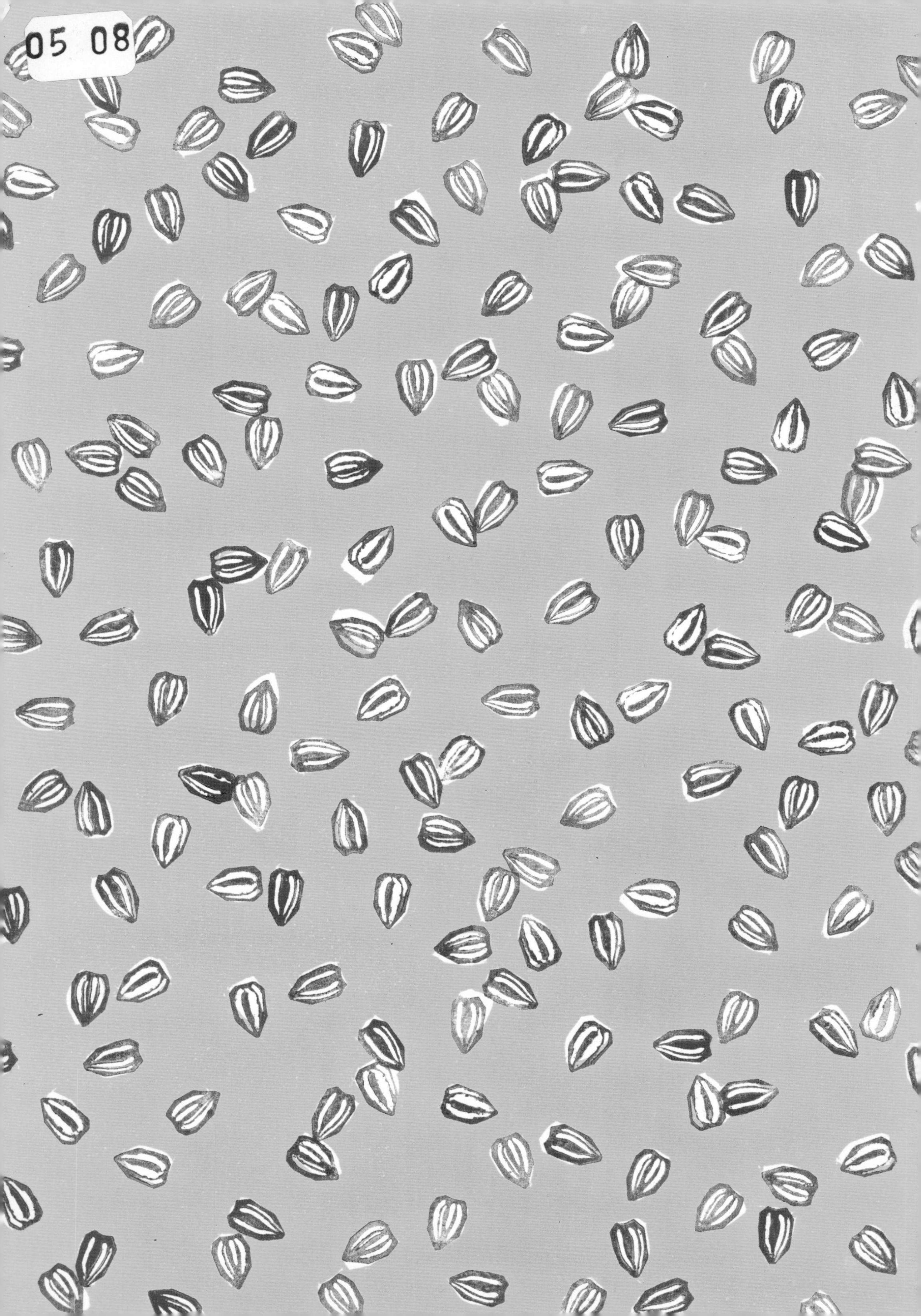
05 08